23

Oh, Lewis!

Story and pictures by Eve Rice

MACMILLAN PUBLISHING COMPANY
New York

Macmillan Publishing Company
866 Third Avenue, New York, NY 10022
Collier Macmillan Canada, Inc.
First published 1974; reissued 1987
Printed in the United States of America

10 9 8 7 6 5 4 3 2 1

The text of this book is set in Plantin.
The three-color illustrations were prepared as pen-and-ink line drawings, with overlays in wash for green and red.
The Library of Congress has cataloged the first printing of this title as follows:
Rice, Eve. Oh, Lewis!
[1. Winter—Fiction. 2. Clothing and dress—Fiction] 1. Title.
PZ7.R36220h [E] 73-19057 ISBN 0-02-775990-3

For my mother and father

One cold winter day, Lewis and his mother
and his little sister Ellie went on a shopping trip.

They walked down the street and as they walked,
Lewis's boots went "thump, thump, thump"

…and then “jangle, jangle, jangle.”

"My boots are unbuckled,"
said Lewis and he stopped walking.

“Oh, dear,” said Mama. “Those boots never stay buckled.”
She bent down and buckled them up again.

"Now I wish they would stay buckled," she said.

And Lewis and his mother and Ellie started to walk again.

They came to the bus stop. As they waited, Lewis felt very cold. Then he saw that his jacket was unzipped.

"My jacket is unzipped."

"Lewis, why doesn't your jacket ever stay zipped?" Mama asked.

"I don't know," Lewis said
as his mother zipped up his jacket.
"This time I wish it would stay zipped," Mama said.

Finally the bus came, and Lewis and his mother and Ellie got on. They rode the bus for blocks and blocks.

Mama looked down
and saw that Lewis had no mittens on.

"Where are your mittens?"
"I don't know," said Lewis. "I think I lost them."
"You are always losing your mittens," said Mama.

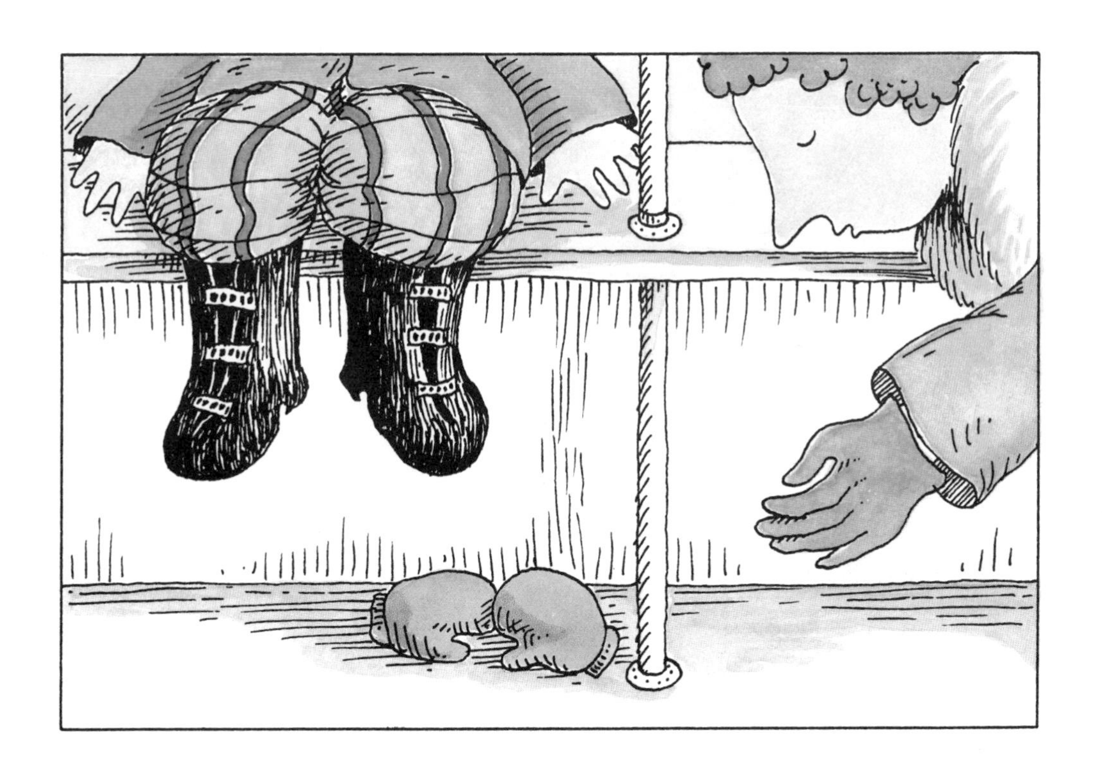

She looked under the bus seat and saw Lewis's mittens.

"Here they are," she said as Lewis held out his hands. "And I wish you would keep them on."

The bus stopped. Mama and Lewis and Ellie got down, but as Lewis stepped from the bus, his hood fell off.

"My ears are cold. My hood is untied."

"You are coming all undone," said Mama
as she tied Lewis's hood back on his head.
"I wish your hood would stay tied and I wish
you would not come undone anymore."

They all went into a bakery.
Mama bought bread and cake,
and a cookie each for Lewis and Ellie.

Then they went to the butcher's
and bought meat for dinner.
And the whole time, Lewis stayed all done-up.

They got on the bus and went home again.

When they were inside, Mama said,
"Take off your coats and boots,
and then we will all have hot tea
and a slice of chocolate cake."

Ellie came in and sat down at the kitchen table.

Lewis came into the kitchen but he still had his coat and boots, hood and mittens on.

"Now nothing will come undone," he said.
"My hood and my boots
and my jacket won't come off."

"What about your mittens?" asked Mama.

"I haven't tried them yet," said Lewis.

"Well, if you take off your mittens first,
maybe everything else can be undone more easily."

Mama was right.
When Lewis had his mittens off,
he could unbuckle his boots,
untie his hood and unzip his zipper.

“Now we can have our tea and chocolate cake,”
said his mother.
Lewis picked up all his things
and put them on a chair.

Then Mama and Lewis and Ellie sat down
to eat their tea and cake,
and Lewis had two slices
because he had had a very hard day.

23